Write the missing numbers on the players' jerseys.

Spot the differences between the two pictures.

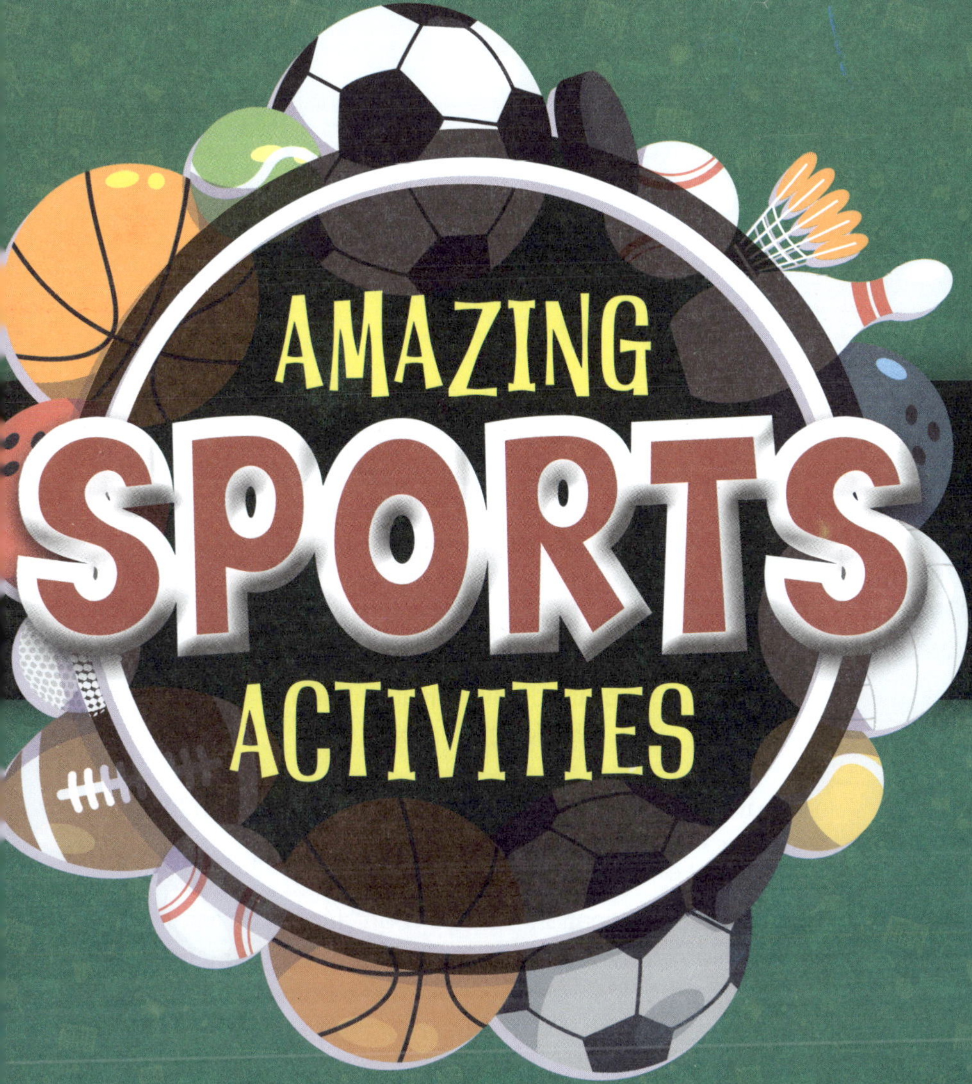

AMAZING SPORTS ACTIVITIES

Published in Moonstone
by Rupa Publications India Pvt. Ltd 2023
7/16, Ansari Road, Daryaganj
New Delhi 110002

Sales centres:
Prayagraj Bengaluru Chennai
Hyderabad Jaipur Kathmandu
Kolkata Mumbai

P-ISBN: 978-93-5702-378-8
E-ISBN: 978-93-5702-451-8

First impression 2023

10 9 8 7 6 5 4 3 2 1

Printed in India

Can you circle the odd one?

Recount the 5 times table and help John connect the basketballs accurately.

Help the football player reach the goal through the green maze.

There are two pictures that are exactly the same. Tick both pictures.

Connect those footballs to the player whose answers are 10.

Look at the picture below and copy it in the grid.

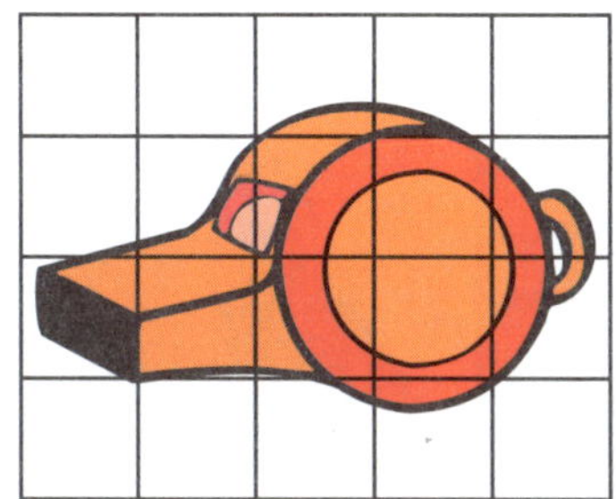

Looking at the options, find and write down the missing parts of the picture.

Write the correct answer in the box

Can you circle the odd one out?

Brightly colour the picture.

The number line will help you find the missing numbers. Let's start....

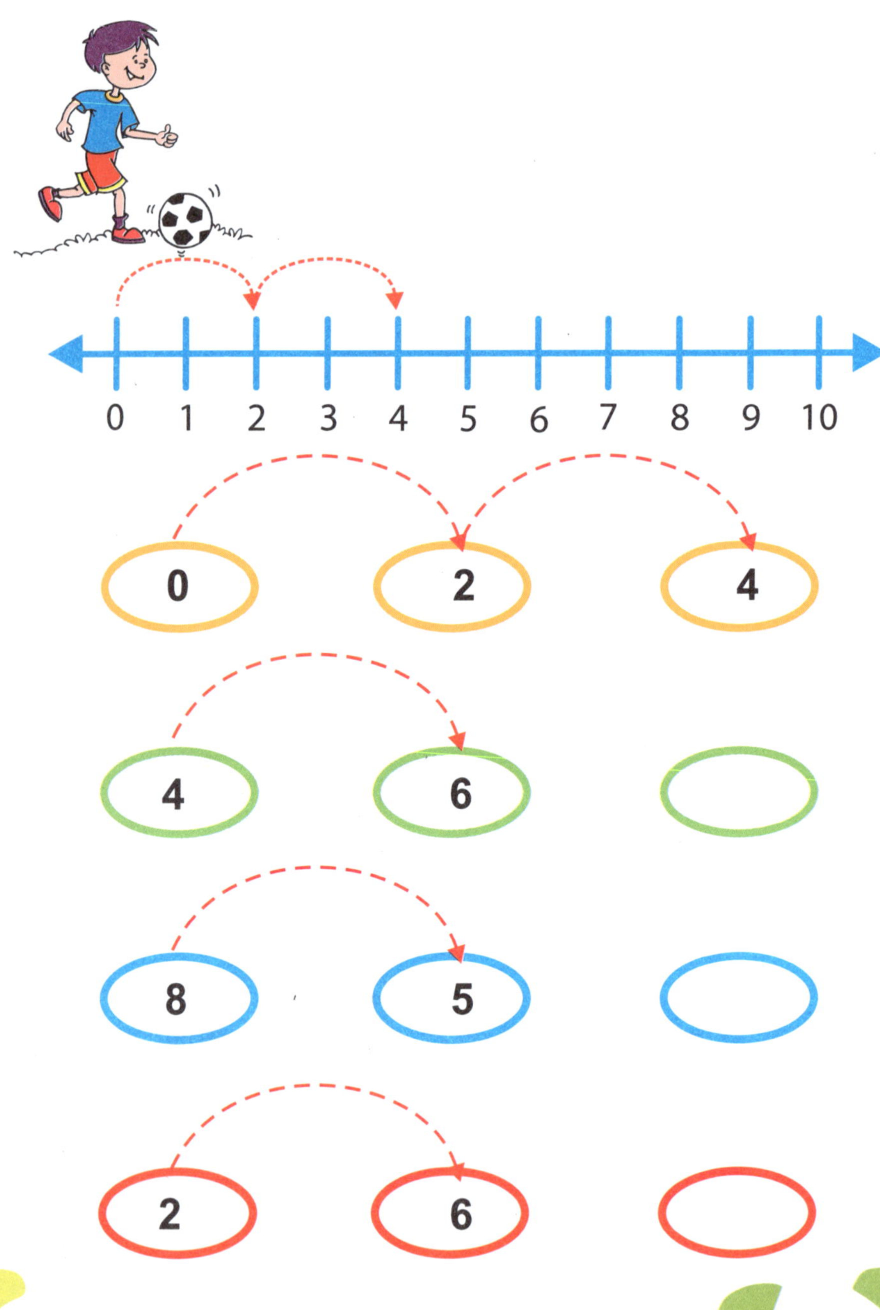

How many objects are there in each box.

Join the dots from 1 to 10 and colour the picture brightly.

Each child's name begins with a particular letter
Trace the route of the strings and find out.

Colour any two boys to make 10.

Decode the pictures and solve the sums.

Calculate the sums, and then colour all the even numbers with blue colour and odd with red colour.

Work out the problems and then match the footballs to their respective answers.

**John has finally found his football.
Help him retrieve it.**

Complete the picture of Mr. Ball.

Colour the picture using the codes given below.

1 =   2 =   3 =   4 =

5 =   6 =   7 =   8 =

Colour the picture brightly.

How many players are there? Count and match.

Colour the picture as shown.

Pick the odd one out.

Find the total number of footballs.

Shade the players according to the colour of the footballs.

Kids, let's have fun!
Find two balls that add up to 5 and colour them in similar colours with your favorite crayons!

Can you help the boy reach the net? Guide him through the maze and let's see if you can do it!

Hey there, little ones!
Count the objects and match them with the right numbers.

Count, subtract and write the answer.

12 – 5 = ☐

Draw a line to match the boy to his shadow.

Make the player look complete. Trace and colour it.

Connect the dots from 1 to 35 and complete the picture of the football player.
Add colours to make it stunning!

Circle the footballs whose answers are 15.

Solve the math problem.

Spot the differences between the two pictures.

Trace the lines and write the correct number in the circle.

Count and write the total number of footballs in the picture.

Draw the picture in the grid.

Do you think you can direct the player to his correct football?

Circle the number that is equal to the number of boys in the box.

Draw a circle around the number that equals the number of boys in the box.

Brighten up the picture with colours.

Help John reach his football and fulfill his football-playing dream.

Colour the complete picture using the number codes 1 to 5.

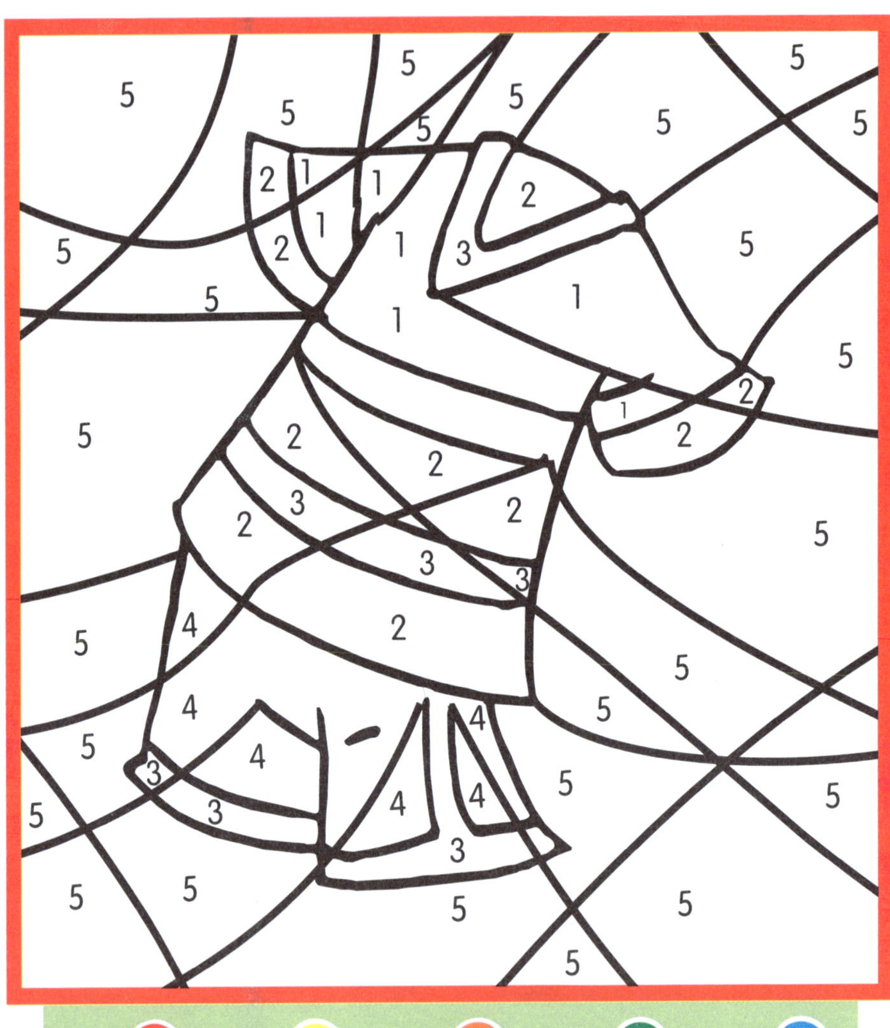

1= 2= 3= 4= 5=

Draw a line from the red balls to the red net.
Circle the net that has the most balls.

Take the appropriate jigsaw puzzle to its correct place.

Identify the jumbled pieces and place them in order.

There are two pictures that are exactly the same. Circle the two pictures.

Help the boy reach the net through the maze.

Colour the circles to pass the ball to your teammate.

Help the boy reach the football through the maze.

Spot the differences between the two pictures.

Solve the math puzzle.

7	+		=	12
+		+		+
	+	4	=	
=		=		=
8	+		=	

Count and tick the total number of objects.

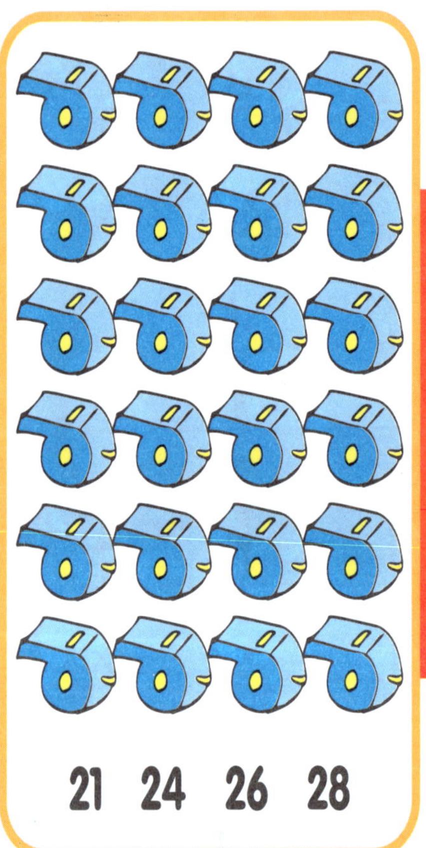

Write the number that comes between the given numbers on each boy's shirt.

Look at the codes of players and then add them up together.

 = 2

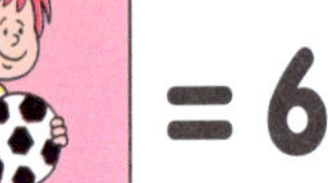 = 6

 = 5

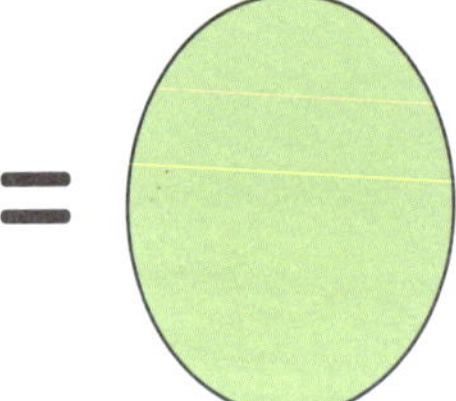

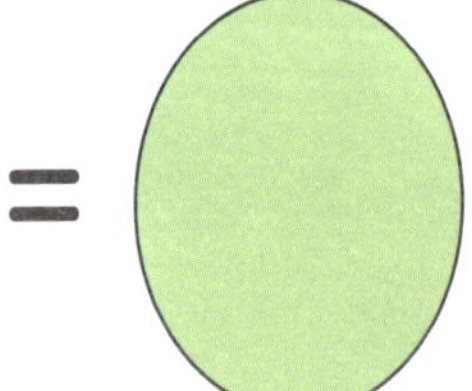

Football fever is in full swing! Tom is enjoying playing football. Colour the picture.

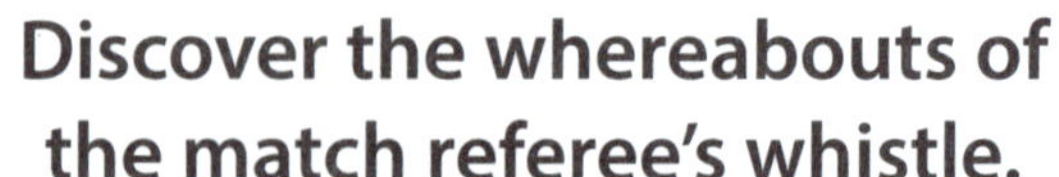

Discover the whereabouts of the match referee's whistle.

Arrange the picture pieces in their proper sequence.

Circle the smallest picture in the set.

Fill in the numbers while looking at the number pattern.

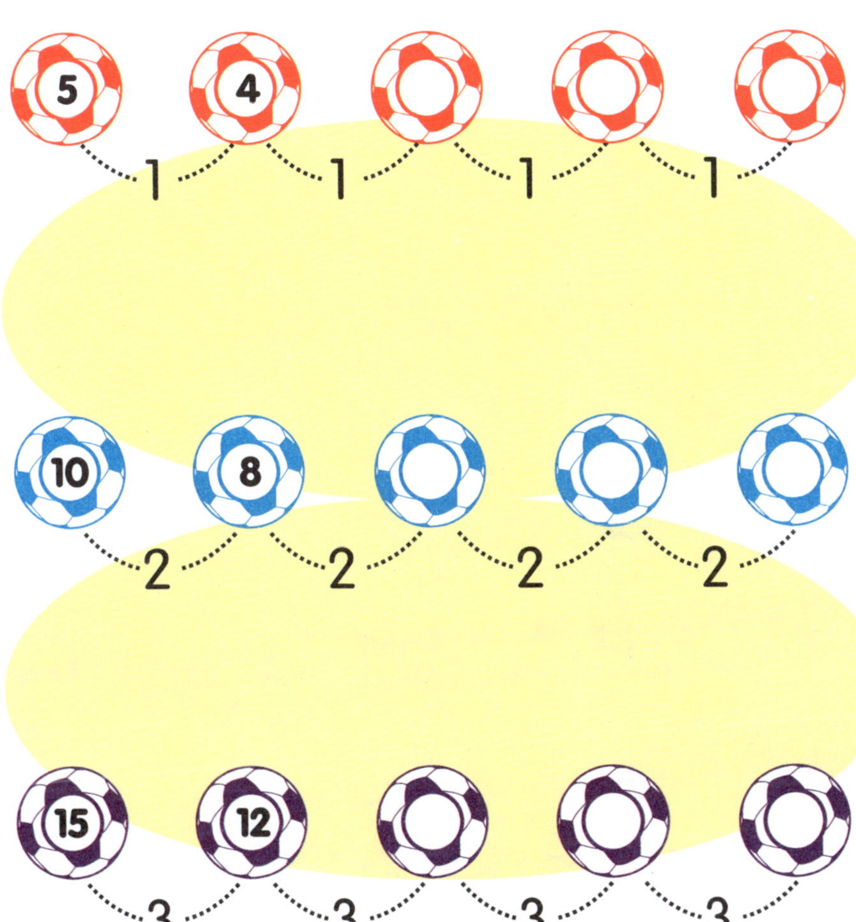

Count and write the total number of football studs in the circle.

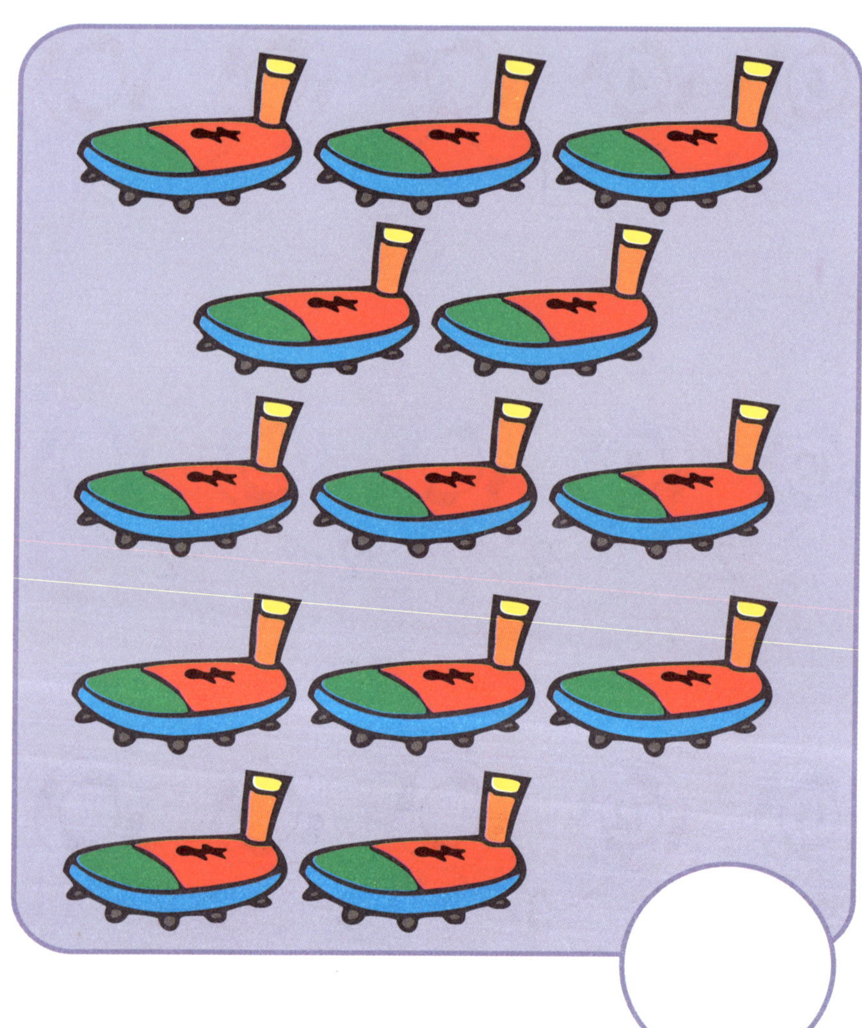

Join the dots from 1-22.
Colour the picture brightly.

Colour the picture in bright colours.

Match the sums to their respective answers.

Find the correct number of pictures. Count and write the answers in the boxes.

Let us help John, to count the number of foot-balls. Hint: Before counting, take a pencil and shade all the footballs.

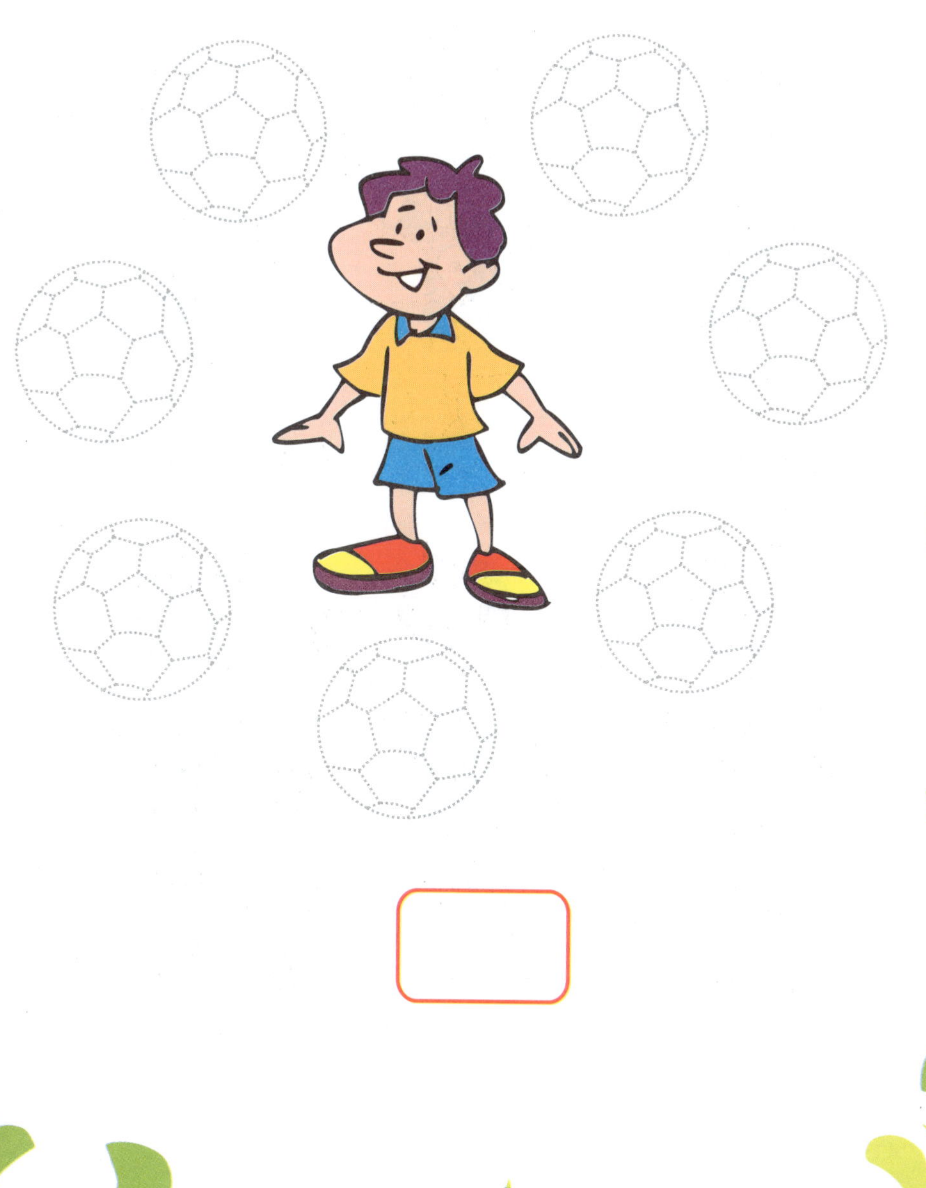

Circle the correct number of players and colour it, too.

Circle the differences between the two pictures.

There are two pictures that are exactly the same. Circle those two pictures.

Neo loves playing football. Help him reach the net through the zigzag maze.

Colour the picture brightly.

Count and write the total number of boys.
Then, write half of that number.

Trace the dotted lines and circle the player who has scored the most goals.

Help the little boy reach his football.

Can you help the boy reach his football, through the maze.

Circle the shadow that is the exact copy of the boy.

Find the differences between these two pictures.

Connect the dots from 1 to 10 and complete the picture.

Count the T-shirts according to their colours and write down the answers.

Red T-shirts ☐ Green T-shirts ☐

Draw a line to match the answers to their multiplication.

6x2 2x5 4x2

Colour as many pictures as indicated by the number given.

Brightly colour the black and white picture.

Help the boys fill in the missing numbers.

5		3	=	2
–		+		
3	+		=	5
=		=		
	x	5	=	10

	+	6	=	11
+		+		+
6	+	5	=	
=		=		=
	+		=	

Learn the art of drawing. Take a pencil and draw a bigger football shirt in the blank grid.

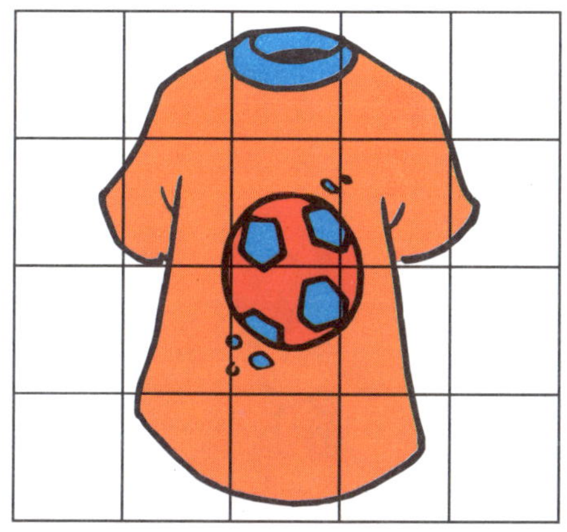

Look at the numbers and fill in the blanks.

a. Which number comes just after 4? __________

b Which number comes just before 8 ? __________

Colour the boy who has the highest number on his jersey.

Write the total number of players in the set.

Write the total number of players in the set.

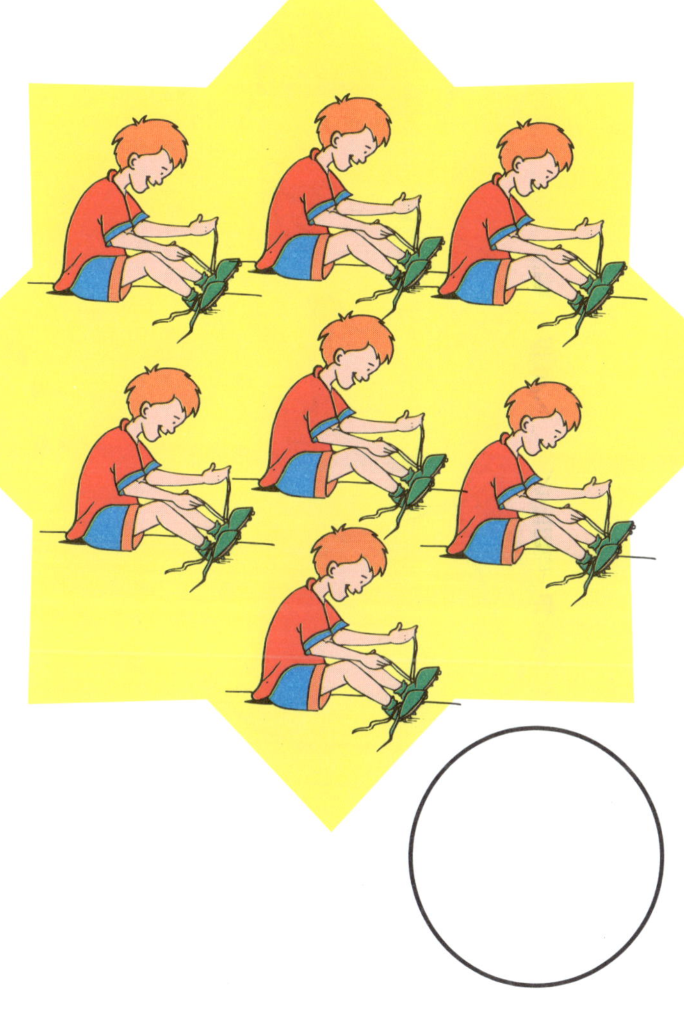

Join the dots and colour the picture brightly.

Trace the path of each string to its football.

Challenge yourself and find the missing jigsaw puzzle.

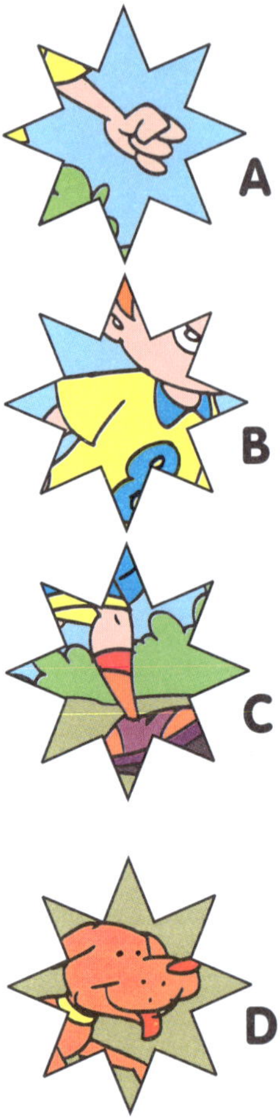

A

B

C

D